The Beautiful Mermaids Series

Yuya's Adventures

Written by

Carmen Melendez-Gutierrez

Illustrated by

Ashley Gallagher

The Beautiful Mermaids Series
Yuya's Adventure

iUniverse books may be ordered through booksellers or by contacting:

iUniverse
1663 Liberty Drive
Bloomington, IN 47403
www.iuniverse.com
844-349-9409

Because of the dynamic nature of the Internet, any web addresses or links contained in this book may have changed since publication and may no longer be valid. The views expressed in this work are solely those of the author and do not necessarily reflect the views of the publisher, and the publisher hereby disclaims any responsibility for them.

ISBN: 978-1-6632-0834-7 (sc)
978-1-6632-0836-1 (hc)
978-1-6632-0835-4 (e)

Library of Congress Control Number: 2020916993

Print information available on the last page.

iUniverse rev. date: 09/24/2020

Special Thanks to

My daughter Gloriani for helping me with editing, my daughter Monica who inspires me, my niece Monica who always listens and supports my crazy ideas, my niece Shannon for her kindness and awesomeness, and sweet Kiara Nicole who originally motivated me.

I dedicate this book to my little sister *Annie Melendez*, who just went to be with The Lord. Thank you dear sister for your lifelong friendship and inspiration. You will be forever in my heart.

Once upon a time
under the sparkling deep end
of the Caribbean sea, there
lived a lively pod of mermaids.

Amapola
the Queen
had two daughters and two
granddaughters who all
lived in the same pod.

They also shared
their pod with 327 of their
closest cousins and friends.

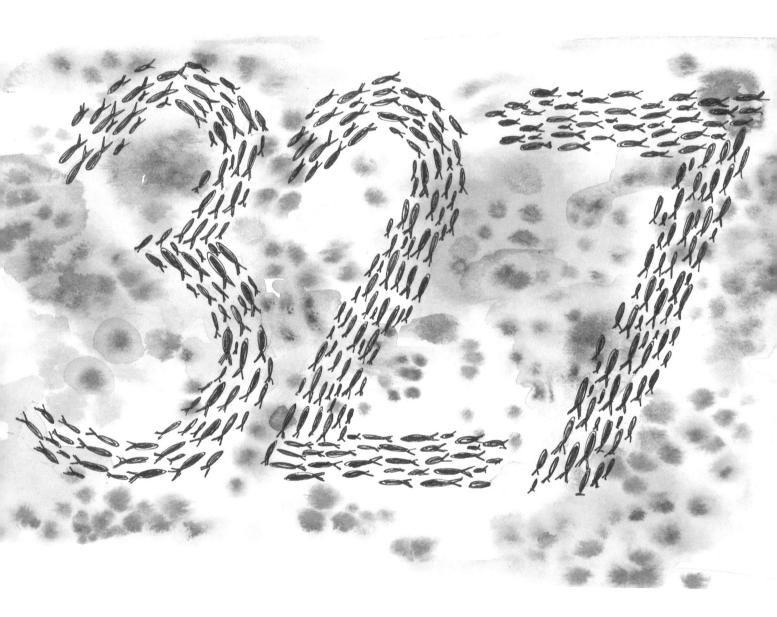

They had a BIG fish family and it was full of LOVE!

Yabucoa the oldest daughter likes to change her tail and her hair every week. She really loves to dress up.

Jayuya,
Yuya for short, was the
youngest daughter, she was
very adventurous. She loved
to swim for miles, exploring
every cave she finds.

One day while swimming, Yuya discovered a cave unlike any she had ever seen before. So, she bravely went in.

Yuya swam and swam through the sometimes dark and scary and sometimes crystal clear waters of that cave. All while not knowing what would be on the other side.

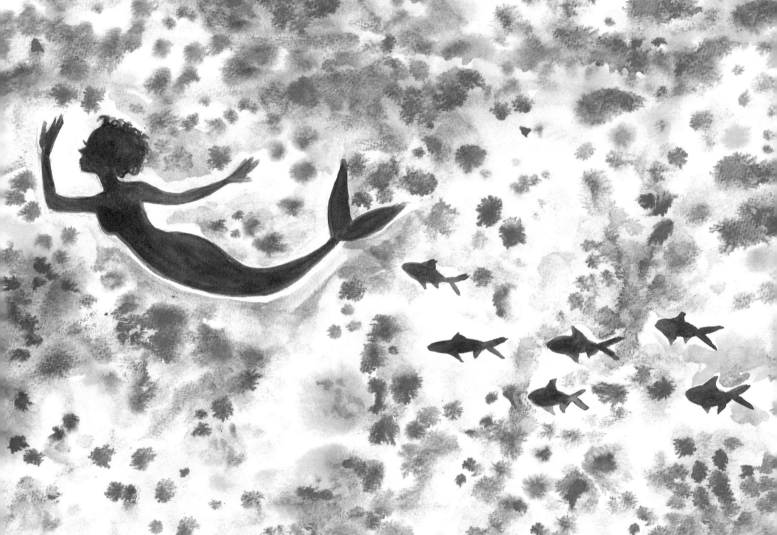

One thing for sure,
she was so fascinated with the
beautiful fish she encountered.

After what seemed like hours, Yuya came out of the cave to the surface of the ocean and near a shoreline.

She saw a group of young children playing on the sand. As she became closer to shore, suddenly shy Yuya hesitated...

She really wanted to talk to the kids, She was a bit nervous but found her courage and approached the children asking them what happened to their fins. To her surprise, she learned they never had fins. Yuya made friends with the kids and had so much fun playing.

As the colorful sun
began to set, Yuya realized
it was time to go home.

On the way home
she got a bit distracted
looking at all the pretty
fish and got lost.

She encounter a shark who offered to take her home, but she kindly replied "No thank you, I don't go with strangers." and she kept on swimming.

She found a sting ray who offered to take her home, but she kindly replied "No thank you, I don't go with strangers." and she kept on swimming.

Just as Yuya was starting to panic she saw one of her best friends, a seahorse named Comerio who was on his way back to his own pod.

Comerio and Yuya easily found their way home.

Amapola was happy to see her youngest daughter. She was a little worried when she didn't answer her shell phone.

And so, Queen Amapola and Yuya went back to their castle where they ate delicious "arroz con gandules" and "tostones".

They even planned to go back and meet the strange fin-less guppies, but that is a "tail" for another time!

The Beautiful Mermaid Series
goal is to bring a lesson on every book

Lesson Learned on this book:
Friendship

No matter who you are, you can be friendly with others that are different to you. Is good to make new friends, especially those that are not like you, but always let your parents know where you'll be. If you have a cell phone, use it. If your phone is running out of battery and you do not have a way to recharge, call your parents or someone who can tell them where you'll be before you run out. Let someone know. Always stay in touch!

laslindassirenitas2@gmail.com

About the Illustrator

Ashley Gallagher is an artist from San Diego, Ca. Her work is vibrant, whimsical and nostalgic, inspired by her hometown and electric colors. Ashley enjoys her days painting, gardening and doting on her 2 cats Richard and Buttercup. You can view her work at

smashleyart.com

"El Sol de Jayuya"; The petroglyph of this symbol is found in the town of Jayuya, Puerto Rico. It is a representation of the sun, worshipped by the Taino indigenous people. The sun was believed to be a powerful God emitting strength, health and longevity to its people as it did for their agriculture.

Printed in the United States
By Bookmasters